My First Pony

"Well done, Harry," said Clare. "You've done an excellent job. Right, now for your first riding lesson."

Harry looked at her in amazement. "My – my riding lesson?" he stammered.

"Yes, I reckon you've earned it."

Tessa Krailing

My First Pony

Inside illustrations by Neil Reed

SCHOLASTIC INC.

New York Toronto London Auckland Sydney
Mexico City New Delhi Hong Kong

ISBN 0-439-19419-9

12 11 10 9   4 5/0

Printed in the U.S.A.   40

First Scholastic printing, April 2000

Chapter 1

Hey, Boy!

The sun woke Harry early. He groaned and turned over in bed. No need to get up yet, this was the summer holidays. But it was so quiet. Why couldn't he hear any traffic noise? He opened his eyes – and sat up with a start.

Where was he? This wasn't his bedroom. His bedroom had blue

wallpaper with ships on it, not plain yellow walls...

Then he remembered.

Yesterday they had moved house. Dad had got a new job, working on a farm miles away from where they used to live. They had travelled nearly all day to get here. Their new home was a cottage belonging to Brook's Farm.

Harry jumped out of bed and went over to the window. He had never lived in the country before. It seemed strange not to see any other houses, only fields. It was rather an empty-looking farm, he thought. Not an animal in sight.

"Harry! You awake yet?" Mum called from downstairs.

"Yes, coming…"

He dressed quickly and went down to the kitchen. Mum was busy clearing cardboard boxes off the table. Last night, when they arrived, they had been too tired to start unpacking.

"Sorry, no bacon and eggs," she said. "I can't find the frying pan."

"Doesn't matter," said Harry. "I'm not very hungry."

"Nor am I," said Dad, coming through the back door.

Mum gave him a sympathetic look. "Nervous about starting your new job?"

"A bit." He poured himself a mug of tea.

Dad used to work as a mechanic in a bus depot, but six months ago the bus company had closed down. He'd been looking for a new job ever since. Now, at last he'd found this one, driving a tractor and looking after the farm machinery.

"Still, it'll be nice living in the country," said Mum. "Won't it, Harry?"

"Mmm," said Harry doubtfully. "Except I wish there were animals."

Dad sighed. "I told you, it's not that kind of a farm. Mr Brook grows things, mainly vegetables. If he had cows I wouldn't have got the job."

"I could have helped you with the milking," said Harry.

Mum laughed. "And a fine mess you'd both have made of it!"

Dad put down his mug. "I'd better go up to the house and find Mr Brook."

"Good luck," said Mum and Harry together.

When Dad had gone they started unpacking the cardboard boxes. After a while Mum said, "Thanks, but I think I can manage now. You go and explore."

Harry wandered outside the house. Exploring wasn't much fun on your own, he thought. All his friends were back home. He didn't know anyone here. And this was only the beginning of the holidays, which meant he wouldn't be starting his new school for ages.

Meanwhile he had no one to talk to.

Worse still, he had no one to play football with!

He kicked a stone. It spun down the cart track. *It'll be nice living in the country*, Mum had said. He didn't agree. The country was boring. He'd much rather live in a town where there were shops and cinemas and parks to play in. And people. A place seemed empty without people.

He wandered down the cart track. After a little way it turned right to the farmhouse where Mr Brook and his family lived. To his left was a narrow, winding lane with a high hedge on both sides. He decided to take the lane.

He soon discovered that it didn't go far, but came to a full stop at a gate leading into a field. He climbed on to the gate to get a better view. And that's when he saw something that cheered him up enormously.

Ponies!

Two of them — one big, one small. The big one was a gleaming chestnut, the small one a light golden colour with a thick white mane. Both were busily cropping the grass. Suddenly the smaller pony seemed to sense that someone was watching. It raised its head to look at him.

"Here, pony! Come here," Harry called.

The pony shook its shaggy mane. Its brown eyes seemed to say, *I don't think I know you, do I?*

"It's all right," said Harry. "I won't hurt you. I only want to make friends."

The pony started walking slowly towards the gate.

"We only arrived yesterday," Harry explained. "My dad's come to work on this farm. To be honest, I don't think I like it here much. It seems awful quiet and I haven't got anyone to play with."

The pony came closer. Harry reached out to stroke its nose.

"Do you live in this field all the year round?" he asked. "It must be pretty cold in winter. I expect that's why you've got a wooden shelter."

The pony inspected Harry's empty hand.

"Sorry, I didn't bring any food," said Harry. "Dad told me there weren't any animals, otherwise I would have done."

The pony gently blew warm air on to his hand.

"I like you," said Harry. "I wish—"

"Hey, boy!" A girl came striding down the lane towards him. "What do you think you're doing? Leave that pony alone!"

Chapter 2

Misty and Samson

Harry was so surprised he nearly fell off the gate. Hastily he climbed down and turned to face the girl. She looked quite fierce and had curly red hair tied back in a pony-tail.

"This is private property," she snapped. "You're trespassing."

"I – I live here," stammered Harry.

"So do I – and I've never seen you before in my life!" She glared at him accusingly.

"We – we only came yesterday. My dad's got a job on this farm." He pulled himself together. "I wasn't doing any harm. I only wanted to talk to the pony."

The girl frowned. "Your dad must be my father's new farm hand. Sorry, I didn't know he had a kid. What's your name?"

"Harry."

"Mine's Clare. And the pony's called Misty. She's a palamino." She looked at him in a much friendlier way. "Come inside and meet her properly."

She opened the gate. Harry followed her into the field.

"Misty was my first pony," Clare told him. "The trouble is I've grown too big for her. Do you ride?"

Harry shook his head. He patted Misty's sturdy neck. Now she was close he could smell her warm, horsey smell.

"That's a pity," said Clare. "She'd be just the right size for you."

"I expect I could if I tried," said Harry. "I can ride a bicycle."

"Not quite the same thing, I'm afraid." She pointed to the chestnut pony on the other side of the field. "That's the one I ride now. He's called Samson. You can help me catch him if you like."

"Okay," said Harry.

Catching Samson didn't sound too difficult. The chestnut was standing very still. Clare took a piece of carrot from her pocket and moved towards him slowly, holding her left hand out flat. In her right hand she held a blue head-collar, but she kept it hidden behind her back.

"Here, Samson!" she called. "Good pony, come here."

Samson tossed his head and trotted away.

"He thinks it's a game," said Clare. "He's not going to let us catch him until he's led us a bit of a dance."

Harry soon saw what she meant. Samson led them a merry old dance all over the field. He kept waiting till they came near and then trotted off again.

Suddenly he seemed to get bored and let Clare come close enough to slip on the head-collar. It had a piece of rope attached to it.

She led Samson over to the gate. "Coming, Harry?"

Harry was torn. He wanted to go with Clare, but he didn't want to leave Misty behind in the field. She looked so sad and lonely by herself.

"I'll be back," he promised her. "I'll come and see you again soon."

Misty shook her shaggy mane as if to say *No, you won't. You'll forget all about me, just like Clare does, now that I'm too small for her to ride.*

"I wish I could ride," said Harry. "I wish it more than anything in the world…"

"Hurry up!" called Clare.

Reluctantly he turned his back on Misty and walked away. Clare closed the gate behind them and together they walked Samson up the lane.

"Do you think you're going to like living at Brook Farm?" Clare asked.

Harry shrugged. "I expect I'll like it okay when I get used to it."

"My dad's very pleased your dad's come to work here," she said. "He says your dad's a wizard with machines."

"Yes, he is," said Harry. "He's the best mechanic in the world."

"Mine's the worst," said Clare. "But he's very good at growing things."

At the end of the lane they stopped.

"I'm going to take Samson out for a ride now," said Clare. "You'd better get on home. Bye, Harry."

"Bye, Clare."

He watched her leading Samson towards the farmyard. As soon as they were out of sight he ran up the track and into the cottage.

"Mum! Mum!" he yelled.

Mum's face appeared at the top of the stairs. "I'm up here, Harry. What do you want?"

"Can I have riding lessons?"

"*Riding* lessons?" She came down the stairs looking hot and bothered. "Why on earth do you want riding lessons?"

"There's a pony in the field," he explained. "She's called Misty. Clare – that's Mr Brook's daughter – said she'd grown too big for her. She asked if I could ride and I had to say no. But if I could have lessons—"

"Harry, have you any idea how much riding lessons cost?" Mum said wearily. "We can't possibly afford them."

"I'll start saving up today," said Harry.

Mum sighed. "If you wait a while I'll try to help you. As soon as we've got this house straight I'm going to look for a part-time job."

Harry sighed. It didn't seem likely they would ever get this house straight. Then he cheered up again. "Can I have some carrots, please?"

Mum smiled. "Yes, I think we can afford some carrots."

Chapter 3

Grooming Misty

Harry hung over the farmyard wall, watching Clare brush Samson's coat. "I asked my mum if I could have riding lessons," he told her. "She said they cost a lot of money, so I'm going to save up."

"Good idea," said Clare.

"What are you doing?" he asked.

"I'm grooming him," said Clare. "Brushing keeps his skin in good condition."

"Do you ever groom Misty?"

"Yes, about once a week. It's hard work because she loves rolling in the mud." She put down the brush and looked at Harry. "Would you like to groom her now?"

He couldn't believe his luck. "Yes, please!"

"I've just about finished with Samson, so we'll take him back to the field and fetch Misty. Wait while I get her head-collar." She disappeared into the stables and came out with a small red head-collar. "Here, you take this and I'll bring Samson."

They walked together up the lane.

"Why do you keep them in a field?" Harry asked. "Why don't you keep them in the stables?"

"It's much better for them to live outside," said Clare. "Ponies are natural grazers. They love being free to eat grass and run around."

"But isn't it cold for them in the winter?"

"In the winter they live in the stables and go out in the paddock during the day," Clare explained. "In the summer it's the other way round. They live in the paddock, but if the sun gets too hot I bring them into the stables."

They found Misty waiting for them, her head poking over the gate.

"She heard us coming," said Clare. "Don't let her see the head-collar or she may run off."

Harry hid it behind his back. "Doesn't she like the stables?"

"Oh, yes. But she likes the paddock better." Clare opened the gate. "We must catch her before we set Samson free, or she'll go after him."

Harry fumbled in his pocket. "Here, Misty. Look what I've got."

Misty stretched out her neck, curious to see what Harry had in his pocket. When he produced a carrot she took it and crunched it noisily.

"Slip the noseband over her nose," said Clare. "That's right. Now lift the headpiece into place and do up the buckle."

Misty looked a little startled. She pulled her head back, rolling her eyes, but Harry kept a firm hold of the rope.

"Well done," said Clare. "Now I'll let Samson go."

As soon as Clare took off his head-collar, Samson galloped across the field, kicking his heels in the air. Misty turned her head to watch him, looking envious. Hastily Harry reached into his pocket again.

"Here, give her some of these." Clare gave him a handful of small hard pony nuts. "Carrots are okay, but it's best to slice them up longways. Otherwise they could get stuck in her throat."

Harry held his hand out flat, as he had seen Clare do with Samson. Misty took the pony nuts gently, brushing his hand with her soft, velvety lips.

"Bring her back to the yard," said Clare. "Then you can start grooming her. I warn you, she's pretty mucky."

Back in the yard they tied the rope to a ring in the stable wall. "First you've got to get rid of the dried mud," Clare said. "You'll need this dandy-brush and a rubber curry-comb."

To Harry's surprise Misty seemed to enjoy being brushed. She half-closed her eyes and stood with a blissful look on her face.

Next he had to wipe her eyes and nose gently with a damp sponge, then use a different sponge to clean under her tail.

"That was the easy bit," said Clare. "Now you'd better go over her with the body brush."

Harry had never worked so hard in his life! By the time he finished brushing Misty he was hot and sweaty, but at last her coat was free of mud. Finally he had to clean out her feet with a hoofpick and paint her hooves with some special oil to prevent cracking.

He stood back to admire his handiwork. Misty looked quite different from the mucky little pony he had brought into the yard an hour ago. She held her head high and arched her neck, as if to say *You see? I can still look good when somebody takes the trouble!*

"Well done, Harry," said Clare. "You've done an excellent job. Right, now for your first riding lesson."

Harry looked at her in amazement. "My – my riding lesson?" he stammered.

"Yes, I reckon you've earned it."

Chapter 4

First Lesson

Harry could hardly believe his luck. He went quite pink with excitement.

"Come with me," Clare said, "and I'll show you where I keep the tack."

He followed her into the stables. "What's tack?" he asked.

"The stuff you have to put on a pony before you can ride it," said Clare.

"Saddles and bridles and stirrups and things like that. They're kept in the tack room."

The tack room had a lovely smell of leather. Harry looked round at all the equipment hanging on hooks and stacked on benches. He hadn't realized riding was such a complicated business.

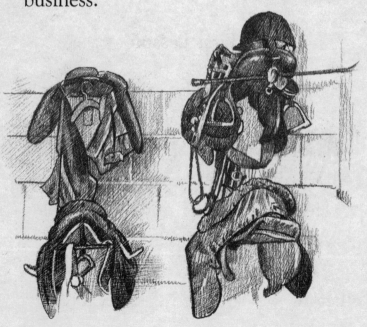

"You take Misty's bridle," Clare said, handing it to him. "And I'll bring her saddle."

They went back into the yard. Clare showed Harry how to place the saddle over Misty's back and fasten the girth under her belly.

"Make sure it's firm but not too tight," she said. "You should be able to get three fingers underneath. I warn you, she'll probably hold her breath and let it out afterwards."

Harry made sure he could get three fingers between the girth and Misty's belly. Then he fastened the buckle.

"Now for the bridle," said Clare. "Hold it in your right hand and put your left thumb into the side of her mouth where she hasn't any teeth. Squeeze gently and when she opens her mouth slip the metal bit inside."

Very carefully Harry did as Clare instructed. To his surprise the metal bit slipped in quite easily. Misty chomped on it with her big square teeth, but she didn't seem to mind.

"Good," said Clare. "Now pull the headpiece over her ears and do it up."

Harry fastened the bridle. "Doesn't it hurt her, having that bit of metal in her mouth?"

"Only if you pull too hard on the reins," said Clare. "Right, Misty's all tacked up, but how about you? Your jeans are okay, but show me your shoes. I hope they've got good thick heels, otherwise your feet will slip in the stirrups."

That morning Harry had nearly put on his trainers. But they were new and he hadn't wanted to get them muddy, so by a stroke of luck he had put on his old school shoes instead. He showed them to Clare.

"Fine," said Clare. "But you must

have a crash cap. With a bit of luck my old one may fit you. I'll get it from the tack room."

She disappeared and came back with a hard hat. Harry put it on. "It feels funny," he said as she fixed the strap under his chin.

"Never mind," she said. "It'll do until you can buy one of your own."

"Can I get on Misty now?" Harry asked impatiently.

"Not until you've checked the girth again," said Clare. "If it isn't done up firmly enough the saddle could slip round and you'll end up on the ground."

To his surprise Harry found that he could get his whole hand inside the girth. "Look at that!" he exclaimed. "It was much tighter before."

"I warned you she holds her breath."

Laughing, Clare moved the girth up another hole and pulled down the stirrups. "Hold on to the saddle and I'll give you a leg up."

Harry put his hand on the front of the saddle and got ready to jump. But at that moment Misty moved slightly and he was left hopping around on one foot.

"Misty, stand!" Clare commanded. "Try again, Harry. One, two, three, UP!"

Harry sprang into the air and landed on his stomach across the saddle.

"Swing your right leg over," said Clare, "and try to sit up."

At last Harry managed to sit upright in the saddle. He looked down at the ground. Although Misty was only a small pony he felt very high up. Her ears twitched as if to say *Who is this person sitting on my back?* He leaned forward cautiously to give her a reassuring pat.

Clare adjusted the stirrups. "Put your feet in and see if they're about the right length. Your heels should be slightly lower than your toes. Now sit up straight."

Harry sat up stiff and straight as a board.

"You're too tense," said Clare. "Relax, you're quite safe."

He didn't feel very safe. It wasn't a bit like riding a bicycle. A bicycle wasn't alive. It didn't keep tossing its head or shifting around like Misty did.

"We'll start with some balancing exercises," said Clare. "Stroke Misty's neck and see how far forward you can reach. Good. Now try to turn round in the saddle until you can see her tail."

After a few more exercises he began to feel safer. "Can we do some proper riding now?" he asked.

"All right," said Clare. "If you feel wobbly hold on to the saddle."

She led Misty slowly round the yard.

When he had got used to the walking movement she made him do more balancing exercises. Next she taught him how to stop by pulling gently on the reins, and how to start by nudging Misty's sides with his legs and saying, "Walk on."

"Right," she said. "I think we'll stop there."

"Oh, do we have to?" said Harry, disappointed.

"That's quite enough for your first lesson." She showed him how to dismount.

Safely back on the ground he felt very excited and pleased with himself. "Thanks, Clare," he said. "That was amazing!"

"You haven't finished yet," she said.

"You've got to untack her and brush her back where the saddle's been. Then you have to do one more important thing."

"What's that?" asked Harry.

"Thank Misty for being so patient. She's your real teacher, not me. You should never forget to thank your pony."

Harry untacked Misty and put the saddle and bridle back in the tack room. Then he put on her head-collar and took her back to the field. As he set her free he whispered, "Thanks, Misty. You're the best teacher I've ever had."

Misty tossed her head and trotted off to join Samson.

Harry sped home. He couldn't wait to tell Mum what had happened.

Chapter 5

Pony Mad!

During the next two weeks Harry had a riding lesson every day. In return he worked hard, grooming and mucking out and putting fresh water in the water trough. The worst part was cleaning up the droppings in the paddock, but Clare said this had to be done regularly because ponies wouldn't eat soiled grass.

The best part was that Misty was getting to know him and look forward to his visits. She whinnied when she heard him coming down the lane and tossed her head when he opened the gate. He gave her a handful of pony nuts and patted her bony nose. She didn't even seem to mind when he put on her head-collar.

"Do you know what I think?" he said. "I think you're glad I came to live here. It must have been pretty boring before, just standing around in this field."

Misty tossed her head again and nuzzled his pocket.

"Sorry," he said. "No more treats now, not till after my riding lesson. Then Clare says I can give you something special, something you like a lot. Come on, let's go and get tacked up."

The most difficult lesson was learning to trot.

"It's – ever – so – bumpy!" Harry complained as he jiggled up and down on Misty's back. He noticed the pony's ears were laid back, as if she wasn't enjoying it much either.

"Remember what I told you," said Clare. "Hold on to the saddle if you think you're going to slide off."

Harry held on to the saddle but he still felt like a bag of jellybeans being bounced around. He began to get the giggles – and once he started he couldn't stop.

Clare sighed. "'You'll find it more comfortable if you rise up and down," she said. "Count ONE-TWO, ONE-TWO, rising on ONE and sitting on TWO. It's what we call the rising trot."

"ONE-TWO, ONE-TWO, ONE-TWO," counted Harry as Misty trotted round the paddock. Clare was right, it was more comfortable. Soon he was going UP DOWN, UP DOWN as if he'd been doing it all his life. He noticed that Misty's ears were now pricked forward, as if she too found it more comfortable.

Compared with trotting, learning to canter was easy. It was just like sitting on a rocking-horse.

"You're doing very well," Clare told him at the end of the lesson. "I think it's time we went for a proper ride."

"A proper ride?" Harry went pink with pleasure. "You mean leave the paddock and go out in the country?"

Clare nodded. "Tomorrow I'll saddle up Samson and put a leading rein on Misty. Then we'll take the bridle path over the Downs. Now, shall we fetch Misty's special treat from the kitchen?"

Misty's special treat was a strawberry ice-cream! She licked it delicately at first – and then golloped down the wafer cone in one huge swallow. The blissful look on her face said, *Oooh, that was delicious!*

"You deserved that treat," Harry told her, "for teaching me to ride."

After his first ride out in the country Harry could talk of nothing else.

"Misty kept stopping to eat grass," he told Mum and Dad at supper. "But Clare said I had to be really firm with her. So every time we came to a clump of grass I shortened the reins and said 'Walk on, Misty.' And she did!"

"Fancy that," said Mum, giving him an extra helping of chips. Riding always seemed to make him hungry.

"Tomorrow the farrier's coming," he went on. "Do you know what a farrier is?"

They shook their heads.

"It's a posh word for a blacksmith. Clare says ponies have to have new shoes every six weeks, otherwise they get sore feet."

"They sound worse than children," said Mum.

"Clare's entering a gymkhana at the end of the month. She's going to jump Samson. And guess what! Clare says I can enter for the Leading Rein class. It's specially for novice riders like me. I don't have to do anything except sit on Misty while Clare leads her round the ring."

Dad laughed. "You've gone pony mad," he said. "Whatever happened to football?"

With a shock, Harry realized he hadn't thought about football lately. He hadn't even missed his old friends. He had a new friend now. She was small and golden and had four legs. True, Misty couldn't play football but she was very good company.

That night he was so excited thinking about the gymkhana that he couldn't sleep. He went downstairs for a drink of water, but when he reached the kitchen door he overheard Mum and Dad talking.

"I can't help being worried." (That was Mum's voice.) "Riding is a dangerous sport. He could get hurt."

Harry held his breath. He knew listening at doors was a bad thing to do, but he couldn't help it. What if they tried to stop him riding Misty?

"It's no more dangerous than riding a bicycle," said Dad. "Anyway, Clare's far too sensible to take him out in traffic until he's more experienced."

"She's very young," said Mum. "And she's not a qualified riding instructor."

"Her father says she's a first-class horsewoman. She's been riding ever since she was three years old. If you ask me, Harry couldn't have a better teacher."

Harry let out a sigh of relief. Luckily Dad seemed to be in a really good mood these days. He liked Mr Brook and he enjoyed working on the farm. He was much happier than when he used to work at the bus depot.

But then he added, "In any case they may sell the pony soon. Mr Brook says it's too small for Clare to ride any more. A pity we can't buy it for Harry, but of course that's out of the question."

Harry was horrified. Sell Misty? No, they couldn't!

He covered his ears and ran upstairs to his room. He wished now he hadn't listened at the door. He'd found it difficult to sleep before – but now it was impossible!

Chapter 6

Gymkhana!

Harry stood in the yard beside Clare, watching the farrier at work.

"Mr Baines knows Misty well," Clare told him. "He brings her shoes ready-made. All he has to do is take off the old ones and make sure the new ones are a good fit."

The farrier heated the iron shoe on

his portable forge and gripped Misty's foreleg between his knees. When he pressed the hot metal shoe to her hoof it made a sizzling sound.

"Is he hurting her?" Harry asked, alarmed by the smell of burning.

Clare shook her head. "What you can smell is just the horn part of her hoof. Don't worry, she's used to being shod."

Mr Baines hammered the shoe into place. In spite of what Clare said, Harry winced every time a nail went into Misty's hoof. But it was true, Misty didn't seem to feel any pain. Every now and then she turned her head to see what Mr Baines was doing, but most of the time she looked rather bored.

"Good girl!" said Mr Baines when he had shod all four feet. "Right, trot her up."

"You can do that, Harry," said Clare. "Lead her up and down at the trot. Mr Baines wants to make sure she doesn't limp."

Harry led Misty up and down the yard. "That's fine," said Mr Baines. "Right, Samson next."

When both ponies were shod Mr Baines packed up his forge and drove off in his van.

"Now we can take them back to the paddock," said Clare.

As they walked up the lane she looked hard at Harry. "You're very quiet today," she said. "Is something wrong?"

He hesitated. All night long he had been trying to work out if he could offer to buy Misty. The trouble was he didn't know how much ponies cost. And then there was the expense of keeping her...

He said slowly, "Clare, do you have to be *very* rich to own a pony?"

Clare laughed. "I'm not rich. But of course I'm lucky because I live on a farm. That means my ponies can live out in the field and eat grass. In the winter they cost more because I have to feed them on hay."

Harry was silent. It wasn't just the food, he thought. Misty would have to be shod every six weeks. And if she got sick he would have to call in the vet...

"Anyway, money's not the most

important thing," Clare went on. "It's the care that matters. Every day you have to get up early and see to your pony before going to school – and again when you come home. It's hard work mucking out stables, especially in the winter. Then there's the grooming ... and the tack to be cleaned ... and oh, a hundred and one jobs to be done. You can't just come home from school and watch television."

Harry swallowed hard. "Dad said you're going to sell Misty. If you do I'd like to buy her."

Clare stopped walking. She stared at him in surprise.

He hurried on, "I thought if I worked hard I could earn the money. Do you think you could wait a bit? Only I don't want you to sell Misty. I don't want her to go away."

"Harry, I'd never sell Misty," said Clare. "She was my first pony and I love her far too much to sell her to strangers. Brook's Farm is her home.

She wouldn't be happy anywhere else.
I promise you, I will never *ever* sell
Misty."

"Oh," said Harry, relieved.

"On the other hand," said Clare, "I
might *give* her to someone."

"Oh?" said Harry.

"But it would have to be someone who lived nearby. Someone who loves her as much as I do. Someone who's just the right size to ride her." Clare looked at him questioningly. "Can you think of someone who fits that description?"

"Me?" said Harry.

"Funny you should say that," said Clare. "It's just what I was thinking."

Harry burst indoors.

"Mum! Mum! You'll never guess. Clare's not going to sell Misty. She's giving her to ME!"

Mum looked startled, but before she could say a word Harry hurried on.

"She says Misty can stay in the paddock … and I can pay for her keep by helping at the stables. She says she was worried about Misty because there was no one to ride her so she's glad I came to live here." He collapsed, breathless, into a chair. "And so am I!"

Mum smiled. "I think we're all glad we came to live here," she said. "Today Mrs Brook asked me if I'd like to help in the farm shop, mornings only. Of course I said yes. I've really missed not having a job. Oh, and you don't have to worry about your clothes for the gymkhana. Mrs Brook says there's a place where we can buy jodphurs secondhand."

At last the day of the gymkhana arrived. Harry felt proud as Clare led Misty round the ring. He had groomed the little pony until her coat gleamed. Her mane and tail were like silk. They didn't win first prize but the judge gave them a special pink rosette because they had tried so hard.

Harry reached forward to stroke Misty's ears. "There's an ice-cream van over there," he whispered. "And I reckon we both deserve a special treat. So let's go!"

The End